JURASSIC WORLD
FALLEN KINGDOM

DINOSAUR RESCUE!

by Kristen L. Depken

Random House 🏠 New York

Welcome to Jurassic World,
the island theme park
that was the home
of many dinosaurs
and prehistoric creatures
that were made by scientists.

They escaped their cages
and destroyed the park.
But now they are in danger.
The island volcano
could erupt at any moment!

The people who used
to work at the park
will go back to save
these amazing creatures.
Let's learn about the dinosaurs!

The *Tyrannosaurus rex*
is almost 20 feet tall
and 40 feet long.
She weighs about 9 tons
and can bite with 8,000 pounds
of pressure!

The last *T. rex* lived
more than 65 million years ago.
It was once the most
powerful dinosaur on the planet.

The Jurassic World *T. rex*
is even more powerful
than dinosaurs of the past.
But she will need help
if the volcano erupts!

Meet Blue.

She is a *Velociraptor.*

She got her name

from the bright blue stripes

on her sides.

The Jurassic World scientists

made Blue using the DNA

of different lizards

and birds of prey.

Blue is the strongest,
fastest, and smartest Raptor
on the island.
She is the only Raptor
who survived when
Jurassic World was abandoned.

When Blue was a baby,
Owen Grady took care of her.
They share a special bond.

This is a *Stygimoloch*.
Her nickname is Stiggy.
She walks on two legs
and eats plants.

Stiggy has a hard skull
that is shaped like a dome
with bony spikes.
She uses her skull to knock
down any creature that gets
in her way.

Stiggy is smaller than most
Jurassic World dinosaurs.
She is less than 10 feet long
and weighs about as much as
an adult human.

But don't let
her size fool you!
Stiggy is very powerful
and very fast.

The *Pteranodon* is a large,

flying reptile.

Their wingspan is as big as

a killer whale!

Their long, pointed beak is

similar to a bird's beak.

The *Pteranodon* uses it

like a net to catch fish.

The *Mosasaurus* is not
an actual dinosaur.
She is a giant sea lizard!
She was once the star
of Jurassic World's
most popular show.

Her many sharp teeth help her
to catch large fish, birds, reptiles,
and even great white sharks.
She has a second set of teeth
to stop her prey from escaping!

Meet the *Ankylosaurus*!

Her name means "fused lizard."

Her body is covered in large,

spiky plates that protect

her like armor.

The *Ankylosaurus* eats
plants and leaves.
She has a club-like tail
that she uses to defend herself
against attacks.

The *Baryonyx* is a fierce
river hunter.
She stands on two legs
and her head looks
like a crocodile's.
Watch out for her sharp teeth!

The name *Baryonyx*
means "heavy claw."
This dinosaur hunts like
a bear, using her claws
to sweep the river for fish.

The *Stegosaurus* has plates
that run down her neck and back.
The tip of her tail
has 4 sharp spikes,
making the tail
a dangerous weapon!

This herbivore has one of the
smallest dinosaur brains.
It is about the same size
as the brain of a dog!

The *Triceratops* was one
of the most popular dinosaurs
at Jurassic World.
Her name means
"three-horned face."
She has two horns on her head
and one on her nose.
The sharp horns
protect the *Triceratops*
during a fight.

A baby *Triceratops* hatches
from an egg the size
of a cantaloupe.
Kids used to ride
the baby *Triceratops*
in the Jurassic World
petting zoo!

Triceratops love to eat plants
that grow low to the ground,
such as ferns.
And they love to be scratched
behind their neck frills!

These are just some
of the many amazing dinosaurs
from Jurassic World!
Will they be saved
before the volcano erupts?